To Catch
a Thief

Halt, adventurer, and read these words before you proceed!

You are about to embark on a journey. To where, only you could possibly say. It is not a journey like any you have been on before, where you start at page one and continue on a straight course until you reach the end. Instead, you will be presented with many choices along the way. Each time you are faced with one such choice, make your decision from the options given and then follow the directions to proceed. Once your quest has come to an end, either favorably or, as I'm afraid in some instances it is foretold to, gruesomely, return to the beginning and start again.

This is not a journey for those who prefer to sit back and let others make the tricky decisions. This is a journey for a leader, a true hero. One who is not afraid to explore the depths of Skullport, steal from a beholder, or fight for the freedom of slaves. If this doesn't sound like you, turn back now and forget you ever came this way. But if this whiff of adventure has whet your appetite, then forward with you, my friend. And good luck!

CANDLEWICK
ENTERTAINMENT

DUNGEONS & DRAGONS®

ENDLESS QUEST®

TO CATCH A THIEF

MATT FORBECK

Y ou little thief," the hooded noblewoman says as she leans over you, your hand caught in her vise-like grip. "You've finally tried to rob the wrong person, haven't you?"

She sounds more amused than angry, but you wonder if the luck you've relied on for most of your life has finally run out. As you gaze up at the woman staring back at you from under the cowl of her voluminous cloak, you realize you've just tried to pick the pocket of none other than Laeral Silverhand, the Open Lord of Waterdeep. If you'd known, you'd have kept walking—maybe all the way out of the city.

You cast about for a way to break free from her, but you see that a patrol of the City Watch (Waterdeep's combination local police and militia force) now has you surrounded. Their leader—a rough-looking woman with the middling rank of civilar—makes a gesture, and two of the blades working for her race up and hold your arms tight as cold-iron shackles.

"I didn't do anything!" you say. You might as well be protesting that the half-moon shining between Waterdeep's rooftops is the noonday sun.

"I suppose a grimy halfling like you had your hand in Lord Silverhand's pocket to help her scratch an itch?" the civilar says with a haughty laugh.

You do your best to look innocent as you give Lord Silverhand a heartfelt shrug. She seemed like an incautious noble who'd wandered into the wrong part of town, and you thought you'd teach her a gentle lesson in why she should keep a better eye on her coinage. It seems she's going to be your professor tonight instead.

"I tripped!" you say with as much honesty as you can fake. "I apologize for steadying myself on her, but surely that's no crime!"

With a wry smile, Lord Silverhand shakes her head at you the way your mother used to when she caught you with your hand in the cookie jar. There will be no lying your way out of this, you can tell.

"Haul this one off to the prison in Castle Waterdeep," the civilar orders the men of the City Watch who surround you. "And quickly! We have bigger fish to fry tonight."

"It strikes me, Civilar Jaulso, that our little friend here could help us with that," Lord Silverhand says. She gazes into your eyes. "You seem like a loyal and dutiful citizen of Waterdeep, after all, don't you?"

"I love Waterdeep more than anything," you say, eager to please. You're not sure where she's going with this, but if it's anywhere other than jail, you're game to hear more.

"I had something stolen from my home tonight."

"I didn't have anything to do with that!" you protest. "I have an alibi!" Or you will, if your pals back at your favorite tavern hold up their end of your standing bargain.

"Don't be stupid," Jaulso says. "The item was stolen by members of our local Thieves' Guild—of which you're clearly not a member—and it's already in the hands of their master, the Xanathar."

You blanch at the mention of that name. The Xanathar is the title of the leader of Waterdeep's legendary Thieves' Guild. That alone would make him dangerous enough, but the current occupant of that position is a beholder, a floating creature about a yard across with a single eye in its middle and ten eyestalks, each of which can cast a deadly spell, splayed around it. It seems you don't get to be the Xanathar without being incredibly powerful to start with.

You gaze up at the Open Lord of Waterdeep and swallow hard. Now you know where she's heading with this. "And you need me to get it back?"

Silverhand nods. "It's vitally important that we recover it, and we could use the help of someone embedded in the underworld, knowledgeable about its ways but not loyal to the Xanathar. Someone like you . . ."

You eye her suspiciously. "What was stolen?"

She purses her lips as though she is not going to tell you and then spits it out. "A baby griffon."

Try to bluff your way out! Turn to page 6 . . .
Refuse to help. Turn to page 9 . . .
Agree to help. Turn to page 17 . . .

You lead the Watchers into a more desperate part of town, and you spot Sully, a low-down friend of yours, skulking in an alley. You start to head in his direction, but Jaulso balks. "This looks dangerous," she says.

You scoff at her. "You think the sort of people who steal baby griffons keep to the best parts of town?"

She frowns but nods for you to proceed. As you do, you secretly give Sully a signal, and he disappears into the darkness.

You follow him with Jaulso's hand on your shoulder. She squeezes it tight, making sure you know that she's not about to let you go. That lasts until you get about halfway down the alley.

Something moves at the end of the alley, blocking off the light. Jaulso curses, and you look back to see that the way you came in has been blocked too. The Watchers send up a cry, but they're already surrounded.

You spin about, kick Jaulso in the shin, and run back the way you came. No one stops you. You emerge into the moonlit street and then stop to see what happens.

The walls of the alley ring with the sound of clashing blades and anguished cries. A moment later, it's all over, and Sully emerges from the darkness, flexing his bruised knuckles.

"You owe us," Sully says. "Beating up Watchers is bad for business."

"I didn't want you to hurt them!" you protest. "I just wanted to break free."

"You should leave town until the heat dies down," Sully says as he sheathes his weapon. "I know about a job for someone with your particular talents. Robbing a dwarf tomb near Neverwinter."

"Do I have a choice?" you ask.

Sully snickers. "Not once you walked down that alley."

THE END

W ait!" you say to Lord Silverhand. "A baby griffon? I know about that!"

This is actually the first you've heard about a baby griffon even existing inside Waterdeep, much less being stolen from the estate of one of the city's lords, but Silverhand and her friends here don't know that. At least you hope so.

Jaulso glares down at you suspiciously. "And how is that?"

You give her a knowing chuckle. "You don't make a score like that without someone knowing. The tongue of every thief in town has been wagging about it."

"Then we hardly need your help, do we?" the civilar says.

"But none of the rest of them know where your little birdie is, do they?" you say with a gleam in your eye.

Lord Silverhand gazes deep into your eyes. "You wouldn't lie to me about such a thing, would you?"

"How stupid would I have to be to do that?" Inwardly, you ask yourself the same question. "If you would just follow me, I can take you right to the terrible tyke."

Jaulso sneers down at you and cocks back her arm to strike, but Silverhand stays her.

"All right," Lord Silverhand says to you as she sizes you up. She decides that she has little choice. She turns to the civilar. "Jaulso? The city has other needs that require me to return to my manor. Take your blades and investigate this quickly. Report back as soon as you can." With that, she turns on her heel and disappears into the night.

The civilar scowls at you. "We are desperate enough to have to trust you, but mark my words: if this is a trick, you will live to regret it—but not for long."

You swallow hard as you wonder what you've gotten yourself into. You've come this far, though, and there's no turning back now. "Just follow me," you say. "It's not too far at all."

Jaulso puts a heavy hand on one of your shoulders and presses a knife against your back with the other. "Proceed."

Run! Turn to page 12...
Teach the civilar a lesson. Turn to page 14...

Y ou want me to steal a baby griffon back from a beholder who happens to be the head of the most powerful Thieves' Guild in all Faerûn?" You shiver at the idea. "I think I'd be better off in jail."

The civilar bashes you across the chin. "You seem to have mistaken Lord Silverhand's request for a request."

You spit blood and glare up at her. "I think we were both quite clear."

Lord Silverhand intervenes on your behalf. "Such violence is hardly necessary, Civilar Jaulso."

"Fine," Jaulso says with an angry slash of her hand. "Toss the little thief in our dankest cell to rot!" she orders her men.

You shout in protest, but you've already made your decision and they've made theirs. No matter how many second chances they might offer you, there's no way you want to go up against the Xanathar, much less the entirety of the Thieves' Guild. Which means they have no use for you at all. Which means you're going to jail.

Despite your history of crime in Waterdeep, you've never actually been caught before. Well, not captured, at least. You normally stuck to crimes like burglary that tended to keep you and your victims well apart. You curse yourself for indulging an impulse to steal what you thought was a noble's purse just to prove you could do it. And for not being fast enough to get away once you were spotted.

The Watchers are as unforgiving as the iron cuffs they fasten to your wrists. They bang you around as they march

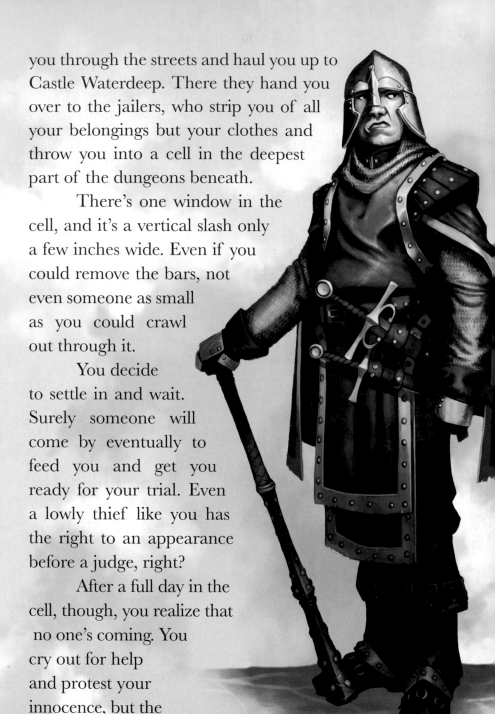

you through the streets and haul you up to Castle Waterdeep. There they hand you over to the jailers, who strip you of all your belongings but your clothes and throw you into a cell in the deepest part of the dungeons beneath.

There's one window in the cell, and it's a vertical slash only a few inches wide. Even if you could remove the bars, not even someone as small as you could crawl out through it.

You decide to settle in and wait. Surely someone will come by eventually to feed you and get you ready for your trial. Even a lowly thief like you has the right to an appearance before a judge, right?

After a full day in the cell, though, you realize that no one's coming. You cry out for help and protest your innocence, but the other prisoners—who sound rather far away—only laugh at your words.

Eventually you decide to save what little there is left of your voice. Is this really to be your fate? To die of thirst for having the temerity to try to steal the purse of the Open Lord of Waterdeep?

Admittedly, that was incredibly dumb, but should something so simple be a capital offense?

It rains that night, but none of the water drips into your cell. It's as if the gods are tormenting you for your arrogance. As the days pass by, you grow weaker—too weak to even call for help anymore—but no one comes for you. Not in time.

A week later, Jaulso remembers you and comes down into the prison to check on you, but it's too late. Your remains are tossed into the waters outside the castle to feed the sharks that patrol there.

THE END

You lead the civilar and her blades on a winding path that eventually takes you to the Market, an open square filled with scores of stalls, carts, tents, and people hawking wares and services of every imaginable kind.

"How much longer?" Jaulso growls. "My patience is thinning by the second."

"Not long at all," you say as evenly as you can manage. "In fact, we're right where we need to be."

She glares out into the square, searching for whatever it is you're talking about, and you take advantage of her hesitation to stomp on her foot and make a break for it. She tries to maintain her grip on you, but there's a reason you wear a cloak with a breakaway clasp.

You leave her holding your empty cloak as you dash into the last vestiges of the crowd still buzzing through the Market even at this late hour.

Turn to page 15...

You hustle the Watchers into the one part of town to which you never venture. As you go, you spy the Watchers following you disappearing one by one.

"I don't like this," Jaulso says to her blades. When she turns and notices the two of you are alone, she gasps in surprised horror.

"I avoided joining the guild till now, but you finally forced my hand," you tell her. "Leave. Forget you know me. If you're lucky and you move fast, your Watchers might rejoin you back at your precinct house."

She spins on her heel and runs.

A goblin emerges from the shadows and chortles at the fleeing civilar. You want to join in her laughter, but your heart's not in it.

"It's not all bad," the goblin says.

"You're a terrible liar," you tell her before you follow her into the dark.

THE END

You might be able to escape from the Watchers, given the opportunity, but then you'd have to spend every second of the rest of your days in Waterdeep glancing over your shoulder. You have a better idea, one that not only gets you off the hook for tonight but makes sure that you won't have to worry about Jaulso and her friends afterward either.

The problem is that you can't take on the Watchers by yourself. There are just too many of them, and the entire city is under their control. The solution to a problem of this scale is going to require help. Lots of help.

You lead the Watchers around in a meandering path for a while, but Jaulso fast becomes impatient. "Where exactly are you taking us?" she demands.

You stop and glance around for a moment before you make a decision and dart off in a new direction.

Find some friends to help. Turn to page 4 . . .
Let the Thieves' Guild teach the civilar a lesson. Turn to page 13 . . .

Jaulso orders her blades after you, and they launch themselves into the maze-like Market, determined to bring you down. You laugh as you dart and turn and duck between stalls and under carts. There are a lot of places in which the City Watch might be able to run you to ground, but the Market isn't one of them.

Eventually, you find an edge of the Market and emerge from its shelter without a single Watcher anywhere near you. You take off as fast as your feet will carry you and disappear into the night.

At first you consider heading for your bolt-hole of a home, but you don't want to risk having the Watchers track you down there. You'd be much better off leaving town while your luck is still holding so you orient yourself toward the nearest city gates and head straight for them instead. It's time to hit the road.

THE END

A baby griffon?" You try to keep the shock from your voice but fail. "Does it bite?"

"Yes, but I'd worry more about the claws," Lord Silverhand says offhandedly, the way you might describe the qualities of a particular meal. "Even on a baby, those talons are far sharper than the beak."

"The ones on the back claws or the front ones?" You've never tangled with a griffon, and you don't really care about the details of how it might dismember you. You're really just stalling for time.

Lord Silverhand can see straight through your pathetic efforts to distract her. She gives you a half-amused smile.

"A griffon has the front half of a giant eagle and the back half of a lion," she says. "What difference does it make which end it uses to tear you apart?"

You rub your chin as if you're considering your decision, even though you've already made it. As dangerous as the griffon might be, disappointing the Open Lord of Waterdeep is sure to be a great deal more troublesome — or so you believe.

"I, ah, think I can help you with that. There should be a sizable reward for the creature's return, right?"

The civilar smacks you in the back of your head. "The only reward you'll receive is to keep your worthless hide out of prison!"

You consider showing the woman the pointy end of your knife, but Lord Silverhand waves her off. "That's enough, Civilar Jaulso!"

The civilar backs away, grumbling. Clearly she'd prefer to deal with you far more brutally than the lord would like her to.

Lord Silverhand turns to you. "If you manage to retrieve the little griffon and return her unharmed, rest assured that I can be quite generous in my gratitude."

You hold back your urge to scoff at her. To think that you might trust in the generosity of a noble—even one as famous and powerful as the Open Lord—might be a bit much, but you don't need to bring her wrath down on you by openly mocking her. If you have the griffon in hand, though, that should be enough to shake loose something from the lord's pockets. At least that's what you tell yourself.

You rub your head and glare at the civilar. Reward or not, you rationalize, chasing the little monster down certainly beats going to jail. Especially since you're not sure that you'd even make it that far in Jaulso's custody.

You give the lord your best smile. "That's good enough for me. So, what's our first step? Has the Xanathar issued any demands yet? Some sort of ransom for the griffon's safe return, perhaps?"

Lord Silverhand shakes her head. A deep frown creases her brow. "He seems bent on keeping the creature."

You sigh in disappointment. "So he's just going to keep the little tyke indefinitely? Seems like this problem just might take care of itself. Won't the griffon eventually grow large enough to eat him?"

"He'll take the time to train it to be loyal to him," Jaulso says. "We believe he wants to raise it as a mount for one of his lieutenants. Imagine the havoc such a creature could wreak upon our populace if it was left under the Xanathar's control."

You grimace as you give up on the idea that the lord might be able to wait the thieves out. It looks like you don't have much of a choice but to help the City Watch find the griffon. At least if you want to live in Waterdeep and remain outside of one of its fine prisons.

"All right," you say. "I'll do it. I'll find your little griffon, and I'll bring it back home. But you're going to have to give me some space to work."

"So you can run off on us?" Jaulso says with a snarl.

"You want me to start poking around the Thieves' Guild, right? How many thieves do you think are going to be caught dead talking to me if I waltz up to them with the City Watch on my tail?"

Jaulso opens her mouth to protest, but you cut her off. "If you think they won't see you coming, you're wrong!"

"He has a point," Lord Silverhand says.

You give them your "Mom likes me best" grin. "You're going to have to trust me," you tell the lord. "At least a little bit. Otherwise, this is never going to work."

"Fair enough." She bends down and gazes right into your eyes. "Don't give me cause to regret it." Then she turns to Jaulso. "I assume you can take it from here? I need to return to my manor."

The civilar gives her a firm nod. "You can rely on us!"

Start asking questions around town. Turn to page 26 . . .

Ask the civilar what you should do. Turn to page 28 . . .

20

"Then it's settled," Jaulso says in the kind of final tone that you usually only hear when someone in her position tells you "You're under arrest."

"I suppose it is," you say. "Unless I can come up with a better idea."

The civilar glares down at you, sure that you're just trying to waste her time. To be fair, you are hoping that a bit of delaying might work in your favor, but perhaps it's not such a wise idea to be so obvious about that in front of her.

"I guess not," you say with a shrug. "If only Marune the Masked can get the job done, then Marune the Masked I shall be!"

Jaulso favors you with the kind of smile your parents would give you when you proved you weren't as stupid as they'd feared.

You rub your chin. "The only question is exactly how I should go about it. . . ."

Wear a disguise. Turn to page 31 . . .
Be yourself. Turn to page 33 . . .
Find a wizard to disguise you. Turn to page 36 . . .

You explain your predicament to Volo, and he listens with rapt attention, stroking his beard as you speak. When you're done, he sits back to ponder your story, and after a moment, takes a long sip of his drink then speaks. "It seems like there's been a rash of disappearances recently. Everywhere I go, people who are missing things. . . ."

Then he sits forward and slaps the table between you, causing you to jump. "The trouble, young'un, is that you're looking in the wrong place! If the Xanathar has this terrible infant you speak of in his nefarious custody, then he's sure not to leave the little tyke up here in Waterdeep proper, where the City Watch might find it and have him at their mercy.

"No, a resourceful creature like the Xanathar hasn't lived this long by exposing himself to such danger. As soon as he laid hands on the beast, he would have taken it to his headquarters in Skullport!"

You groan at the idea of having to travel to such a dangerous place, but you instantly know that the man is right. "By all the gods, I don't want to have to venture into such a dark and dank den of villains."

Volo scoffs at your fears. "It's not such a far way to go for a stalwart little one such as yourself. Adventurers manage the journey all the time—every day! After all, Skullport is merely a few levels down the very Undermountain atop of which this fair city was built!"

You know about Skullport all too well, even though you've never actually been inside it. People in Waterdeep talk about it all the time. It's the sort of place that parents use to scare their children into walking the straight and narrow. It's an entire underground city built inside of a massive cavern through which runs an underground river called the Sargauth. It's a rotten place—often literally, due to the dark and damp—filled with pirates, monsters, and worse.

But you realize that Volo is correct in his estimation, no matter how much you'd rather he wasn't. If the Xanathar has the baby griffon, he's sure to have hauled the creature off to his headquarters in Skullport. Even the City Watch would be afraid to follow the beholder into his lair down there—which probably explains why Jaulso was so eager to press you into her service rather than try to find the Xanathar on her own.

Sounds dangerous. Too dangerous. Turn to page 81 . . .
The den of scum and villainy it is! Turn to page 40 . . .

The pirates seem happy to see you, and you hope that at least they won't kill you like the scum who call Skullport their home might.

"Looks like you've had a bad night," their leader says flashing a gap-toothed grin. "Let us give you a hand up."

Just then, something swims past you and nips at your heel. You decide that whatever troubles the pirates might cause, they have to be better than being eaten alive.

The pirates pull you up onto the dock—and then refuse to let go.

"Thanks very much for all your help," you tell them. "But I have business I need to attend to here."

"That's very funny," the leader says without laughing at all. "We have business here too. With you."

You squirm desperately but find yourself surrounded. There's no way to get past the pirates except by leaping back into the river.

"And what business might that be?" you ask.

"Why, we're looking to expand our crew," the leader says with a wink toward a woman wearing an eye patch with a glowing eye drawn on it. "We all voted, and we decided to take you on!"

Turn to page 55...

W aterdeep's a big city, but a griffon is the kind of thing that attracts attention, even if it's only a baby. One can't exactly wander about with the beast on a leash without getting noticed. Someone has to know something about it.

You take your leave of the civilar, hoping that she doesn't have her Watchers shoot you in the back as you go. She scowls at you until you disappear from her sight, making sure you know that she's never going to let you walk away from this job. No matter what you do, if you disappoint her, you'll be hunted till your last day in Waterdeep, for sure.

Determined to do your best, you head down to your favorite tavern and start asking around about the missing creature. The Halfway Inn is the kind of place where adventurers tend to gather, either to celebrate their latest success or to plan their next dungeon delve. You're not looking for any partners on this particular job, since no one else would be foolish enough to get wrapped up in such troubles, but adventurers are the sort of people who pay attention to things like griffons on a professional basis. If anyone in town is likely to have seen a griffon, it's them.

You run into a sailor who's fresh off a buccaneer's ship that just sailed into the harbor. It's his first time on dry land since he was kidnapped out of Baldur's Gate, a gigantic city far to the south. He seems in a fine mood despite all that, probably because he's no longer on the ship.

"I don't know about no griffon," he says to you. "In fact, I don't know much about this fine city of yours at all. But I was just chatting with someone who seems pretty wise about such things, if you know what I mean. Maybe he can point you in the right direction. Follow me!"

The sailor takes you on a winding route through the tavern, which apparently has more rooms in it than you ever knew. Eventually he stops at a table at which sits an older man with a sharp beard and even sharper eyes. The man shakes your hand and gestures for you to take the chair next to him, then puts aside the tattered notebook in which he's been scratching away with his quill.

"Hello, my new friend!" the man says with a wide and friendly smile. "My name is Volothamp Geddarm, but you can call me Volo. Everyone else does!"

Turn to page 22 …

I admit it," you say to Jaulso. "I've never tried hunting down a kidnapped baby griffon before. I'm at a loss as to where to begin."

"Don't you think you ought to show me that you can be at least somewhat useful before you give up?" she asks with more than a hint of menace in her voice.

"Oh, no, no, no." You shake your head emphatically as you show her the palms of your hands. "I'm not giving up. Not at all! I just wonder if you might have some idea about how I should find this baby griffon of yours."

"You mean of Lord Silverhand's." Jaulso rubs her chin. "Well, if I wanted to meet the master of the Thieves' Guild, I might try to pretend I was someone he knew. Or at least someone he might want to know."

"That's all well and good," you say. "But do you have any idea who might fit that bill?"

"I don't know." Jaulso sighs in exasperation. "You're supposed to be the one with underworld connections here. Aren't you aware of any other thieves who live in Waterdeep?"

"You might recall that I'm not part of the Thieves' Guild," you tell her. "We freelancers prefer to give the guilded thieves their own space. They have a tendency to want to cut us open otherwise."

Jaulso remains unimpressed. "You've heard of Marune the Masked?" she eventually offers.

You give her a cautious nod.

"He's supposedly the greatest thief in Waterdeep, correct?" She continues, not waiting for your reply. "We've been after him forever, but no one even seems to knows what he looks like. . . . "

Seeing where this is heading, you play dumb for the nice civilar, hoping that she might somehow take pity on you. "So?"

"He could even be female. Or a halfling to boot. So what's stopping you from presenting yourself to the Thieves' Guild as Marune the Masked?"

You rattle off a list in your mind that includes the fact that just because you don't know what Marune looks like doesn't mean that someone inside the Thieves' Guild isn't much wiser about the issue than you. Also, you don't especially relish the idea of the journey to the Thieves' Guild headquarters in Skullport. That would mean risking a journey through Undermountain, which you would rather avoid. But you keep your mouth shut and shrug at the civilar.

"Nothing?"

Turn to page 21 . . .

B ut aren't you just perfect the way you are?" Grinda says with a giggle as she reaches down to pinch your cheeks. "Why would anyone ever want to change you?"

You hold back an exasperated sigh and let her continue to think you're a child—who apparently has a dangerous life. "I need to reach the Xanathar, leader of the Thieves' Guild, so I can save the baby griffon, but he won't talk to me. But he might talk to Marune the Masked. . . ."

"Whom no one has ever seen—and so no one knows what he looks like?" she says uncertainly.

"Exactly!"

Grinda scratches her head, and a mouse-sized fairy scampers out of her hair and flitters away. She doesn't seem to notice. "Well, it seems a terrible shame, but assuming I agree to do this for you . . . since no one's ever seen Marune, what should I change you into?"

Slick and dangerous. Turn to page 50 . . .
Slick and dangerous. Turn to page 50 . . .
Tall, dark, and powerful. Turn to page 54 . . .

No need to complicate things. You make yourself a cheap mask out of a black bandanna with eyeholes cut into it, and you darken your hair with handfuls of soot. Even your mother wouldn't recognize you—and if she did, she'd start in right away about how you should have been a doctor like your father and your sister.

"You look like a villain from a bard's tale," Jaulso says.

"With a name like Marune the Masked, what would you expect?"

She shrugs her shoulders. "Fair point. Just try not to get yourself killed out there."

"Aw, Civilar, I didn't know you cared."

"*Before* you recover the baby griffon. After that, you're on your own."

Chastened, you give her a firm nod. "Wish me luck."

"If you don't manage to bring that griffon back for me, you're going to need a lot more than luck."

Turn to page 34…

Well, since no one knows what Marune the Masked looks like, there's no reason for anyone to believe Marune doesn't look like you, right? You decide to walk into the King to Swoon For, a tavern with an entrance to Undermountain, and give it a shot.

"Hey, there," you whisper to the bartender. "I'm looking for a way to get to the Xanathar."

The bartender chuckles. "Who's asking?" she says.

"Marune the Masked," you say as confidently as you can manage. "Perhaps you've heard of me?"

The bartender gives you a sidelong look, and for a moment you think this might all work out. Then she bursts out laughing.

"Is that so funny?" you ask.

She shakes her head at you and then calls out to the rest of the patrons in the room. "Hey, folks! We got another one! Says they're Marune the Masked! What's that? The third one this week?"

You blush bright red and show yourself out. Soon afterward, you realize that you're going to need to leave town to get away from the laughter that follows you.

THE END

N ow, get moving," the civilar says. "Time's wasting."
Admittedly, you were trying to waste time, hoping that the problem would somehow solve itself. "I'm on the case," you tell Jaulso.

"Perhaps I should just throw you straight in jail and save us both the embarrassment of your inevitable failure."

"And waste an excellent costume? I spent whole minutes setting this up!" you say, gesturing toward your face.

She takes a swing at you with her fist, but you scamper out of the way — and keep moving. "Don't get your scabbard in a twist!" you shout over your shoulder as you charge into the night. "I'll have your griffon back in good hands in no time at all. You have my word on it!"

"What good is the word of a thief?" asks the civilar.

You wonder the same thing as you decide where to start your hunt.

Off to Downshadow to recruit some help! Turn to page 38...
Down to Skullport! Turn to page 45...

The ray catches you square, and you expect to fall over dead. Instead, you feel a rush of goodwill toward the Xanathar. You wonder if the two of you might become best friends, but your abject terror of being disintegrated drives you to throw off whatever mind-altering magic he's using.

It does cause you to stagger a bit, though, and you inadvertently step on the little griffon's tail. It screeches and springs into the air with you clutching its back legs.

The two of you glide past the Xanathar's balcony to a safe landing, well out of the reach of the beholder's eyestalks. From there, you race through town and the dungeons above it until you are safe in Waterdeep.

You find Jaulso and her Watchers waiting for you when you emerge into the daytime sun. "I'll take that!" she says as she snatches the griffon from your arms.

"Plus the credit for its rescue, I'm sure!" you say.

"And you get to go home rather than to jail," she says as she stalks off toward the home of the lord who lost a little griffon. "Everyone's happy, right?"

You have to admit she has a point.

THE END

If you're going to survive all this, no regular, handmade disguise will do. You need something magical to help out. Or someone . . .

At Jaulso's suggestion, you look up a wizard by the name of Grinda Garloth. She lives in Mistshore, a run-down neighborhood located along the harbor's north shore. It's so riddled with poverty and crime that the City Watch doesn't even go there, but the civilar gives you the address.

When you knock on Grinda's door—which is set into the hull of a beached ship that was blasted from the sea decades ago—an old woman opens it and glares at you with undisguised disdain.

"I'm sorry," you say. "I was looking for a wizard by the name of Garloth. . . ."

She sneers at you and then yanks you inside and slams the door behind you.

"You can't just stand out there," she says. "What if someone were to see you?"

"Does Grinda live here?" you say, confused.

The old woman smooths her hair and picks a random bug from it. "You're looking at her, honey." She glances up and down at you. "And who am I looking at?"

You introduce yourself and explain your predicament. You need to save a baby griffon from the Xanathar or face some hefty jail time.

She laughs at you as she reaches down to tousle your hair. "That's a charming tale for such a young child to be spinning, but I fail to see how it has anything to do with me."

You don't bother to correct her on her belief that you're a human kid. Instead, you give her your most disarming smile and say, "I was hoping you could help me with a proper disguise."

Turn to page 30 . . .

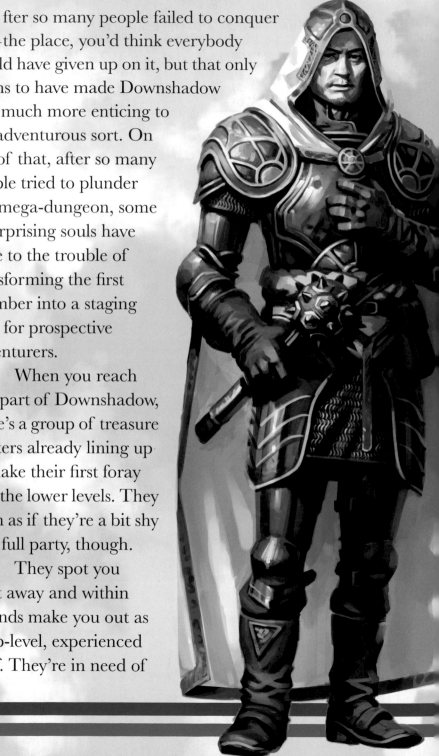

After so many people failed to conquer the place, you'd think everybody would have given up on it, but that only seems to have made Downshadow that much more enticing to the adventurous sort. On top of that, after so many people tried to plunder this mega-dungeon, some enterprising souls have gone to the trouble of transforming the first chamber into a staging area for prospective adventurers.

When you reach that part of Downshadow, there's a group of treasure hunters already lining up to make their first foray into the lower levels. They seem as if they're a bit shy of a full party, though.

They spot you right away and within seconds make you out as a top-level, experienced thief. They're in need of just such a person to round out their crew, and they start to pressure you to join them.

"We need someone to spot the traps for us," their careful cleric claims. "And someone better than our last thief! If she'd been any good at it, she'd still be with us!"

"After this," their fearsome fighter says, "we're planning to head up to Neverwinter, if you care to join us. This old man in the Yawning Portal sold us an ancient map to the tomb of a dwarf necromancer, and we mean to make the most of it."

"Of course, we're going to need someone who can read dwarf runes before we try that," says their wily wizard. "You happen to have any expertise along those lines?"

Turn to page 44...

"Looks like I'm going to Skullport," you say as you bury your head in your hands.

"Good!" Volo says, his enthusiasm undampened by your reluctance to venture into the depths below Waterdeep. "Do you know how to get there?"

"I just have to find my way through a couple levels of the dungeons buried beneath Undermountain," you groan. "I might need to see if I can tag along with some adventurers headed that way. . . ."

"Sure." Volo laughs good-naturedly. "If you want to do it the hard way."

You glare up at him, and he realizes that you don't find his joke funny.

"My apologies! I just assumed someone with your skills would have a half-dozen ways in and out of such a place already mapped in your head, but clearly I was mistaken."

"It's okay," you say as you rise to leave. "I'll find a way on my own."

Volo blushes and puts out a hand to stop you. "Have you heard of the Yawning Portal? It's an inn not too far from here, in the Castle Ward, and it features a passage into the dungeons' upper levels."

You know this. In fact, almost everyone in Waterdeep knows this. "I've used it before," you say, "but it's hardly a direct route to Skullport."

"Of course not," Volo says. "But there's another place around the corner from there that has just such a route. Though it's not for the timid, I'm afraid. . . ."

Heartened to hear that you might not have to brave Undermountain to reach your goal, you slap a hand on the table in front of the man. "Just tell me where it is."

Shortly, you find yourself standing in a night-black alley, handing a gold piece to a hooded man who stares at you with bulging, unblinking eyes.

"You can swim?" he asks.

Unsure why he wants to know, you nod, although you get the feeling he'd take your money whether you would sink like a stone or not. He bites your coin to verify its worth, then opens a hatch set into the wall at the end of the alley, beyond which you see nothing but darkness.

"In you go."

You step up to the edge of the hatch, then hesitantly turn to ask the man a question, but before you can get out a single word, he boots you into the shaft beyond. The shaft is angled—and greased with something you'd rather not think about.

You slide down the twisting and turning shaft for what seems like forever. Just when you begin to wonder if you should try to put a stop to your descent and claw your way back up to demand a refund, you reach the bottom of the slide and tumble into the open!

You plummet through the air and splash into the dark waters of the Sargauth. Spluttering and chilled but unharmed, you swim toward the lights on the shore as fast as your arms and legs will take you. As you near a dock, you spy two groups of people watching you approach. One seems to be a pack of pirates, while the other appears to be composed of the regular kind of scum that lives in Skullport.

Approach the pirates. Turn to page 25...
Approach the regular scum. Turn to page 49...

You don't speak a single word of Dwarvish other than the phrase "I'm sorry, I've made a terrible mistake," but you tell your new friends you're fluent. How are they going to know?

"Are you heading anywhere near Skullport?" you ask to confirm their plans.

"Gods, no!" the wizard says. "That place is full of pirates feeding off each other like piranhas. We're on the hunt for monsters to slay and fresh treasure to bring home."

You consider their plan for a second, as you know it means letting Jaulso figure out how to help Laeral Silverhand rescue her little griffon from the Xanathar's clutches. Then you flash a broad smile and say, "Count me in!"

True to their word, your new pals never get anywhere near Skullport, and that suits you just fine. Sooner or later, you'll join them on their venture up to Neverwinter, but that's a whole other story.

THE END

You need to thank Jaulso for coming up with this crazy plan to impersonate Marune the Masked. You didn't think it was going to work.

Although your intentions are good and you're feeling positive about the power of your disguise, you find yourself heading to the Underdark. Not the subterranean realm known for its strange creatures, but a tavern of the same name over in the Trade Ward. Rather than change course and head straight to Skullport you convince yourself that if or when Jaulso catches up with you, you can tell her you

were trying to find a member of Thieves' Guild topside who you could follow to their secret headquarters in Skullport.

When you get there, the half-elf bartender spots your mask and beckons you over. She seems unsure as to who you might be, but she is willing to hazard a guess. "Marune?"

Never one to pass up a golden opportunity to impersonate someone else, you nod in agreement. "Who else would so brazenly wear a mask in public like this?"

"But why would you come here now?" she asks, confused that someone of your stature would darken her door.

"I have business in Skullport, and I am looking for a way to reach it quickly. I heard that you might be able to help me out in that regard."

The bartender's face cracks with a wide smile. "We happen to have a secret passageway in our basement!" she whispers to you.

You cannot believe your luck. When you'd realized your altered destination, you had been hoping to rest your feet for a bit while you got up the courage for what you had agreed to do. To remain here now would look suspicious. You stifle the urge to cringe at your fortune. "You don't say. Could you be so kind as to permit me to use this route?"

"For the great and famous Marune the Masked? Of course!" The bartender takes you by the hand and leads you into the tavern's back room. In the far corner, she pushes aside a rack of shelves stocked with supplies, exposing a wooden door. She removes a bar on this side of the door and hands you a lit torch from a sconce on the wall, watching you expectantly as you take it.

Beyond the open door, you see a set of stairs leading down into the darkness.

"I'm so excited!" the bartender says. "You'll have to tell me all about your adventure when you get back."

"I certainly will," you say as you venture down the stairs. The bartender closes the door behind you, and you hear the solid thunk of the door's bar falling into place.

Rather than waiting to starve to death in the stairwell, you continue down. After a long hike that meanders deeper and deeper underground, you emerge in the high part of the of Skullport, away from the wide river that runs through the cavern that encapsulates it.

While you're glad to no longer be in the stairwell, you're not sure where you should go next. You cast about for clues as to where the Xanathar might be. There are a few suspicious characters in suspicious situations around you, as there always are in Skullport, but which is worth investigating?

Follow a floating skull. Turn to page 57 . . .
Follow the sound of a crying child. Turn to page 62 . . .
Follow a thief. Turn to page 64 . . .

You swim for the group of locals, and they reach down and haul you out of the river before the current drags you away. They're a motley crew of thieves and murderers: an emerald lizardwoman named Ssslasssh, a gray deep gnome called Fundunsun, and a one-armed crimson tiefling with bright fangs who calls herself Heleen.

Despite their appearances, they seem friendly enough. They snarl at the pirates until they scuttle away, and then they fuss over you a bit and haul you into a nearby tavern called the Blind Fish to get you dry and warm.

Once you're feeling a little better, you start peppering your new friends with questions about the Xanathar and his possible involvement with the disappearance of a baby griffon from a certain lord's estate up above. They glance at one another, and you notice their hands moving for their knives.

"Look," Fundunsun says. "The Xanathar has a very strict rule about people talking about him."

"That'sss right," Ssslasssh hisses. "And thossse who break it in public like thisss are either brave or ssstupid."

"And also worth quite a bit in the way of a reward." Heleen flashes her fangs at you. "It's nothing personal."

Turn to page 60...

C ould you make me look slick and dangerous?" you ask.
Grinda purses her lips and gives you a hard look. "Are you sure about this?"

"No complaints!" you tell her. "I promise."

"All right . . ." She pulls a crooked wand from the sleeve of her dirty blouse and sets to work. She beckons you over to a workbench and pours a silvery fluid into a crucible set atop it. She plucks a gummy substance from a small tin and places it in the crucible. She taps the crucible with her wand, and a bright tongue of fire appears beneath it.

Smoke explodes all around you, and a moment later, you reappear as a small green poisonous frog with bright-red eyes.

"There you go, honey!" Grinda says to you. "Slick and dangerous! Good luck on your quest!"

You flick your tongue for a moment and then hop off to find your destiny.

THE END

I love it!" you say, and you wrap your long arms around Grinda to give her a massive hug. She giggles and blushes like a young maiden with a crush.

"I'm so happy for you," she says with pride. "Now, get out there on your little quest and find that griffon friend of yours, or whatever you're looking for."

You thank her profusely and promise to return to regale her with the story of your success. You may have slipped into Grinda's home as a halfling, but you emerge looking every bit the drow warrior sliding through the night's shadows as if you're nothing but a whisper, gone before you're even heard.

You could get used to this, and you wonder how long the transformation will last. It didn't occur to you to ask. If it's permanent, you don't think you'd mind.

Hoping to find a fast way through Undermountain to Skullport, you make your way toward your favorite tavern, the Yawning Portal, where you expect to be able to pick up some advice. You stride into the place and glance around, looking for someone who might be able to help you. Those who see you gape in wonder, and you realize that perhaps your disguise isn't quite as subtle as you'd hoped.

The drow may be the stuff of legendary adventures, but they're usually on the other end of the sword, at least when tales of their exploits reach Waterdeep. They make their homes in places like Menzoberranzan, the fabled City of Spiders, which sits in the upper part of the Underdark that sprawls beneath Neverwinter, and their patrols are the bane of adventurers searching for treasure everywhere.

The people of Waterdeep don't care for the drow at all, but you feel powerful enough not to care what they think. You may not be among friends, but you're here to worm your way into the Thieves' Guild, not greet your pals. As you approach the tavern's bartender, he gives you a side-eye that makes you wonder if he's reaching for his sword. Despite that, he comes when you beckon him over.

"Drizzt Do'Urden," he says with a scowl. "I thought I told you I never wanted to see you again. It's not safe for you around here."

He's clearly mistaken you for someone other than Marune the Masked. You suppose you should have worn an actual mask to complete the disguise, but you decide to roll with it.

"Show me a fast way to get to Skullport from here, and I will trouble you no more," you negotiate in your huskiest voice.

He scratches his chin and then points to a door at the back of the tavern. You nod your thanks and head toward it. The door opens onto a dark hallway being used as a pantry, which quickly comes to a dead end.

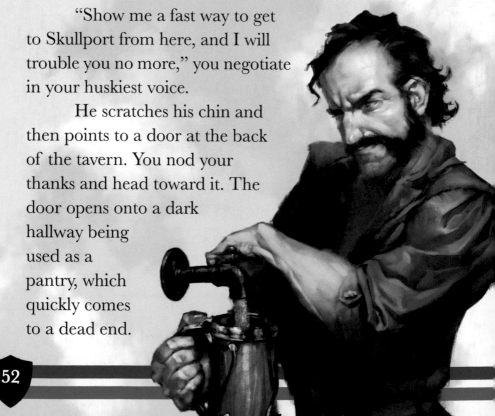

As you search for a secret passage out of the hallway, the door behind you slams shut, plunging the place into blackness. You spin around, blind in the dark, and find a blade rammed straight through your chest.

The last words you hear as your life bleeds out of you are "I told you it wasn't safe, but you wouldn't listen. . . ."

THE END

C an you make me tall, dark, and powerful?" you ask the wizard, daring to hope.

She scurries off to a worktable, beckoning you to follow her. She dumps a bunch of odd things into a crucible and lights a fire beneath it with a tap of her wand. Then she points the wand at you and says a number of things you don't understand.

A moment later, you find yourself much taller. Grinda gives you a fragment of a shattered mirror, and you see that you now have pointed ears and long white hair. You're wearing a suit of blackened armor that makes you look positively dangerous. A drow not to be reckoned with.

Grinda totters up behind you and says, "What do you think?"

Turn to page 51...

The pirate with the eye patch lifts it up to expose a crimson gem where her eye should be. As you gaze into its depth, it begins to glow, and everything fades to black.

When you awaken, the sun beats down on you from high above. You find yourself on the main deck of a creaking ship heading out to sea. You look up to spy a black flag bearing the skull and crossbones flapping atop the mainmast.

A woman appears over you and laughs. "Welcome aboard the *Molly Roger*! You picked a smashing day to join our crew!"

"How's that?" You crawl to a nearby railing and spot a smaller ship off the starboard bow. It's trying to flee from your ship and failing.

The woman leans down and whispers into your ear. "Because you're about to see what pirate life is really like."

THE END

A skull floats overhead, unattached to anything at all, most particularly not a body or a neck. Fortunately, it doesn't seem interested in you. Instead, it's wandering about over the houses of Skullport like it's a mystic, haunting guard on some kind of unfathomable patrol.

You chase after it, thinking that since you're looking for a floating-head-thing (a beholder), a floating skull might somehow lead you to it. It zips about the sky over Skullport, such as it is, moving rapidly from the low rooftops all the way up to the ceiling's apex. You climb on top of a ramshackle building so you can keep an eye on it, trying to remain in the shadows as you do.

The skull keeps moving, getting farther away. You chase it, leaping from roof to roof and keeping it within sight. When you jump onto one roof in particularly awful repair, though, your right foot goes straight through it, and you yelp out loud in surprise and pain.

That's when the skull turns toward you.

While you were following it, the floating skull seemed like more of a curiosity than anything else, but now that it's coming straight at you, it's terrifying. You yank your foot out of the rotting roof, turn, and run.

You dash across the rooftops, doing your best to avoid stabbing your foot through another one, until you realize that as long as you're atop the houses, the skull can see you for sure. That's assuming it can see at all, but despite its lack of eyes, it's doing a fine job of tracking you so far. You need to get out of sight, quick!

You leap down into an alley and sprint off in a random direction. You take several turns through a maze of streets and byways. Huffing and puffing from your race through town, you find a dark corner—well out of the way and plenty distant from where you started out—to sit down in and rest.

The skull lowers itself right in front of you, facing you with its empty eyes, and hovers just out of reach.

"You are new," the skull says with a voice that doesn't come from its nonexistent lips but somehow still rings in your ears. "Are you a wizard?"

Experience has taught you that when someone asks you if you are something, they either need that sort of person or want to kill that sort of person. Either way, you're in trouble. You try to read the skull's expression, but there's nothing there to see.

"I am one of the Skulls of Skullport," the skull says. "Are you a wizard?"

Hesitant and uncertain, you give your best guess as to what the right answer might be. "Yes?"

"Excellent," the skull says, floating closer. It emits a green glow from around its edges. "Prepare to be absorbed."

"Wait!" you shout as you throw up your hands. "That sounds fatal! And painful!"

"The Skulls are beyond pain."

"I'm not a wizard!" you cry. "I lied!"

The skull stops moving toward you, and the green glow around it fades. "You are not a wizard?"

You shake your head emphatically. "I can't even do card tricks!"

The skull gazes at you for a long moment before it speaks again. You're too afraid to move, thinking that it might be about to leave you alone—as long as you don't run. "You shall not be absorbed," it says.

You let out a huge breath you didn't realize you'd even been holding.

"The penalty for lying to a Skull is death."

You shove past the skull and sprint away at top speed, screaming the entire way. The skull isn't quite as tenacious about your punishment as you are about escaping it. Eventually you find a passage to the surface, and the skull fails to follow you.

Once you make it to Waterdeep, you realize that while you've escaped the skull, you've failed in your mission entirely. However, you decide that you can keep using your disguise as Marune the Masked—in another city. Baldur's Gate, here you come!

THE END

W ell, then you shouldn't consider this personal either," you say just before you leap atop the table and kick Ssslasssh square in the teeth. She goes reeling backward and crashes into a nearby table, knocking it over as she falls.

Heleen and Fundunsun swing at you with their knives, but you leap off your table onto the next one, spilling all the food and drink there onto its occupants. They shout at you in protest and take swipes at you with their fists, but they're all far too slow. You hop from table to table like a frog, disrupting as many meals as you can—and angering nearly everyone in the tavern.

For some people, this might be a problem. For you, it's all part of the plan.

Fundunsun jumps after you, trying to follow your mad dash about the tavern. One of the annoyed patrons grabs him and slams him to the table, pinning him there among the spilled drinks.

Heleen charges alongside the tables instead, staying away from the angry patrons, but she can't quite keep up with you. You finally reach the bar and leap over it to hide. She tries to follow, but the bartender sees her coming. He stops her cold with a short club he waves in her face.

"Help!" you scream at the top of your lungs. "Those three are traitors to the Thieves' Guild! They were asking questions about the Xanathar!"

"What?" Heleen cries as the bartender takes a swing at her with his club and narrowly misses. "That's not true at all! You're lying!"

You peer over the top of the bar, happy that it's between you and Heleen, and scoff at her. "How dare you say such things about me? I'm a thief, not a liar!"

The other patrons in the tavern don't seem to care who's telling the truth. "I say we take them in for the reward!" one man says. "All of them!"

Maybe bringing up the Xanathar again wasn't such a great idea, you think, but it's too late now. Rather than having just three people after you, you now have to face down the entire bar. These are not good odds—but they weren't much better before.

The bartender—a white-bearded orc with a patch over one eye—turns his attention to you, and you try to scoot between his legs. He grabs you before you make it too far, and he hoists you up in front of him so he can look you right in the eye. "What's a morsel like you doing here?" he asks with a vicious laugh.

You spit in his good eye and bite his thumb, hard.

When the bartender lets you go, howling in pain, you clamber back atop the bar and spy a window you might be able to leap through.

Go for the window! Turn to page 69 . . .
Never turn your back on a fight! Turn to page 71 . . .

You follow the sound of a crying child, and find yourself drawn through the streets of Skullport. It's not likely to be the baby griffon you're looking for, but you find it hard to turn away from a youth in need. And just what does a crying baby griffon sound like, anyhow?

When you finally track down the noise, you discover a pack of well-armed bugbears watching over a group of bruised and filthy people chained together into a line being herded off toward the docks. There's one child among them. He is about five years old, human, and is wailing at the top of his lungs as he clutches his weeping mother's hand. "You can't sell us to separate people!" the boy says between sobs. "You can't split us up! You can't!"

The lead bugbear—an orange-furred fellow with a chunk missing from his ear—sneers down at the boy. "Shut up," he says with a vicious snarl. "Or I'll give you something to really cry about."

That only makes the boy cry louder, right

up until the point at which the irritated bugbear cuffs the child with the back of his hand, bloodying his lip. The boy clings to his mother tighter than ever, although his wails taper off to whimpers. The slaver gives a satisfied grunt and pushes the mother along.

You glance around, but no one else on the street seems to be paying the scene much mind. Apparently this sort of thing isn't uncommon in Skullport, although the very idea of slavery horrifies you. You decide to follow them at a distance, hoping that you might find an opportunity to do some good, although you're unsure of the exact shape that would take.

Turn to page 68...

Out of the corner of your eye, you've been watching a thief you know from Waterdeep. She's called Peggy, on account of the fact that she has a peg where her left leg used to be. She likes to think she's as quiet and stealthy as the sleekest burglar in the city — even Marune the Masked — but in fact she staggers around making so much noise you can hear her coming from streets away.

Another thing you know about Peggy is that, while she often tries to play herself off like some kind of pirate, she's actually a landlubber and a known member of the Thieves' Guild to boot. If anyone knows where the Xanathar lives

or the location of the Thieves' Guild headquarters here in Skullport, it would be Peggy.

Unfortunately, you can't just go up and ask Peggy for help. After all, she still blames you for the loss of her leg. It wasn't your fault that you managed to outrun her when an owlbear stormed after you both for stealing its eggs.

Well, not entirely.

You decide to follow Peggy to see if she'll lead you anywhere interesting. As long as she doesn't see you, you shouldn't have to worry about her trying to exact her revenge. You stick to the shadows and watch her roam.

She wanders around the city for a bit, stopping in a tavern or three along the way, and eventually she leads you to a posh mansion in the best part of Skullport. As she enters the place, you realize that it's way too nice for a thief as rotten as Peggy to ever be able to afford.

It must be the Xanathar's home. You can't exactly barge in and ask to see the owner, though. In fact, it would be best if you never crossed paths with him at all.

You stake the place out for a while, hoping to see the beholder himself come floating out so you can sneak in during his absence. Eventually, though, you get bored with sitting and watching, and you decide to start poking around. That sort of impulse has gotten you into plenty of trouble over the years, but it hasn't gotten you killed — yet.

As you circle the building, you spy a light on in a large room with a wide balcony that looks out over the rest of the city. You decide that this is as good a place as any to start.

You climb up the wall beneath the balcony and slip onto it as silently as you can manage. You hear voices coming from inside, so you sidle up to the doorway that leads out onto the balcony from the house proper, and you listen.

You hear Peggy talking first. "You lined up a trainer for the griffon? That's great, boss! I never figured you'd manage it that fast."

"You underestimate the kind of pull I have in this city," another voice says. Gravelly, deep, and inhumanly hollow at the same time, it could only be the Xanathar's.

You stifle a shiver and continue to listen.

"So, you want me to bring the trainer down here tonight?" Peggy stifles a yawn.

"This griffon's not getting any younger."

"Is the trainer going to be ready?"

"With the money I'm paying, he'd better be."

You peer through the doorway from the balcony to see a gigantic floating eye petting a little griffon with one of its ten prehensile eyestalks. On a desk beside the Xanathar, there is a huge sack filled with gold coins spilling out of it.

The Xanathar has his back to you, but unfortunately Peggy does not. Her eyes go wide in surprise as she sees you.

Snatch the money. Turn to page 75 . . .
Snatch the griffon. Turn to page 77 . . .

As you near the docks, one of the bugbears glances back and notices that you've been following them through the city. She alerts her leader, who shouts something at you in what you assume is Bugbear but sounds like little more than gibberish.

You don't scare off that easily, though, especially when you're pretending to be Marune the Masked. Instead, you step forward and return the bugbear's snarl with relish. This puts the bugbear back on his heels as he considers how to deal with someone who challenges his authority.

The boy chooses that moment to wave at you. You, seeing no reason not to, wave back.

That's when the other bugbears start to snicker at how their leader seems to have lost control of the situation. He flushes bright red, points at you, and shouts something that has to translate as "Attack!"

Flee! Turn to page 78...
Fight! Turn to page 84...

You crash through the window and find yourself in an alley running behind the tavern. You race down it and lose yourself deep inside Skullport before anyone can follow you. You're still soaking wet and chilled to the bone, but at least no one's trying to press you into service on a pirate ship or turn you over to the Xanathar.

For now, that is. You know you have to keep moving if you don't want anyone else to try to sink their claws into you.

You skulk around the city and realize that no one down here cares how late it is in Waterdeep. The sun doesn't ever shine in Skullport, which means it's always night and no one seems to know when to sleep. The place is constantly humming with activity. It's a city with a pulse that beats faster than a dwarf miner's pickax.

While Waterdeep might be mostly filled with humans, elves, dwarves, and the occasional halfling, Skullport welcomes intelligent creatures of all kinds. The only thing you need to succeed here is power, no matter the nature of your skin. You find a few people warming themselves by a garbage fire, and you sidle up and warm your bones while you think.

You're not going to find the baby griffon by asking around. Everyone who lives in Skullport is either working for the Xanathar or terrified of him. There's only one thing for you to do. You need to go straight to the Big Eye himself.

From what little you know about the beholder, he spends most of his time either at the offices of the Thieves' Guild or hunkered down at his own estate. Both places are

well protected, and you can't expect to just waltz into either of them and steal back a little griffon.

Once you can feel your fingers again, though, you know you need to make a decision. Do you strike at the creature's den or at his place of business?

Head for the Xanathar's home. Turn to page 82...
Head for the headquarters of the Thieves' Guild. Turn to page 86.
..

You've had enough of people pushing you around today. You see Ssslasssh racing toward you, trying to cut off your avenue of escape. She thinks she has you, but she's wrong. You decide it's time to try your luck with an entirely new tactic.

You turn the tables on Ssslasssh and charge straight at her. Your move catches her off guard. She tries to stop her forward momentum, but she winds up skidding toward you. You lash out with a swift kick to one of her knees, and she goes tumbling over the top of you and sliding along the floor.

The lizardwoman spins around onto her back, probably expecting to spy you fleeing toward the tavern's door. Instead, she finds you leaping on top of her and pummeling her with your fists. She tries to fight back, but you refuse to let up. It's hard to tell if you're doing much harm to her green-scaled skin, but you keep at it anyway, punching her again and again until your arms begin to tire.

You don't know how much time has gone by. It seems as if you've been at this for an hour already. When you stop to take a breath, you discover that you've knocked Ssslasssh unconscious. You lean back and rub your aching fists, and then you're rudely reminded that the lizardwoman was not the only problem you brought into the tavern with you.

Heleen appears out of nowhere and clocks you across the chin with her one arm. She packs an amazing punch—causing you to see stars as you go sprawling along the tavern's floor, and slam to a stop against someone's boots. Following them slowly upward you realize they belong to

Fundunsun, who glares down at you with a snarl on his lips as he draws his short sword from its scabbard.

"We should have let the river have you," the deep gnome says as he slashes at you. You dodge out of the way and reach for your own knife. "Or maybe the pirates. They would have at least hauled your carcass out of town."

You don't like to fight like this—or ever, really—and you especially hate having to brandish a weapon. It's a good way to get yourself killed or, nearly as bad, end up having to kill someone else.

Despite being a renowned thief, you're no murderer, and you prefer to keep your hands clean. In Waterdeep, taking out a knife to defend yourself means that everything has gone wrong and you've somehow failed to talk your way out of suffering the consequences.

Of course, you're not in Waterdeep. You let the Open Lord talk you into scurrying down into Skullport for her on a fool's errand, and now it looks as if you might end up on the wrong end of a sharp knife for your troubles.

Heleen snickers as she comes up behind you, brandishing a dagger of her own. You spin about, trying to keep her and Fundunsun from surrounding you as the rest of the patrons in the tavern brawl all around. Keeping an eye on both of them proves a challenge, but you're not about to give up now.

"The Xanathar prefers we bring people to him still breathing," Heleen says. "But it's not really necessary. He can get information out of the dead. It's just a little . . . trickier."

The tiefling stabs at you, and you parry her attack with your blade. While you're occupied, though, Fundunsun slashes at you, and the tip of his sword nicks your side open. You stagger backward, clutching at your ribs with your free hand.

You realize that you're going to have to kill these people to get them to leave you alone — or take your chances in the river again. Your eyes dart toward the doorway, and Heleen moves to cut you off. It's now or never.

Dive into the Sargauth! Turn to page 90 . . .
Fight to the death! Turn to page 89 . . .

You point toward the large sack of gold sitting on the Xanathar's desk, which sits behind the beholder, out of his line of vision. Peggy goggles at you as you sneak your way toward it, but the Xanathar doesn't seem to notice. Maybe beholders can't read humanoid faces all that well, or maybe he's too preoccupied with the griffon to be bothered with someone as lowly as Peggy.

You signal to Peggy that you'll split the money with her if she keeps the Xanathar distracted—or at least doesn't point out to the beholder that you're robbing him. The thief gives you a discreet nod as you creep farther into the room. You don't trust her for an instant, but, wow, that's a lot of gold sitting there—too big a score to just walk away from.

You quietly scoop up the bag, taking care not to jingle any of the coins together. You smile at Peggy, who seems impressed by your skill. Few thieves would even attempt such a thing, and here you are, pulling it off underneath the floating bulk of the Xanathar himself.

Just as you turn to slip out of the building without a trace, Peggy stabs a finger at you and shouts, "Boss! It's a thief! And not one of ours!"

The beholder spins around to see what Peggy is talking about, but you're already on your way out by the time that happens. You knew you couldn't rely on Peggy—just like she probably knew she couldn't believe you—and you were ready to bolt at the first sign of treachery.

She's timed it just right to make it hard on you, though. If she'd said something right away, you'd have just fled. Now, though, you're carrying a heavy sack of coins and have to make it back to the balcony to have your shot at getting away.

As you dash for the balcony, a ray stabs out from one of the beholder's eyes, and the floor of the balcony disappears, saving you the trouble of leaping over the railing.

You would have liked to have saved the little griffon, but that's clearly impossible now—for someone who doesn't want to die. At least the sack of gold you stole should be enough for you to leave Waterdeep behind and set yourself up in a new life far, far away. You hope.

THE END

First you need to cause a distraction from your real plan to buy you time to get to the baby griffon. You slip over toward the desk, signaling to Peggy that you'll split the gold with her if she lets you steal it. The moment you pick it up, though, you know she's going to betray you. Before she has a chance to react, you hurl the open sack straight at her.

She tries to catch it, but it splashes against her chest instead, sending gold coins scattering everywhere. The Xanathar screeches in surprise at Peggy for a moment. While he does, you leap over and snatch up the baby griffon.

"Look at it this way," you say to the beholder. "You're going to save so much money not having to hire a trainer."

"Give me back that griffon!" the beholder says. As you race toward the balcony with the griffon in your arms, the Xanathar fires a ray at you from one of his eyes.

Turn to page 35...

You try to go back the way you came but your retreat has been blocked by a bugbear. As crazy as it seems, it looks as though your best bet is to attempt to charge straight through their ranks. You inhale a long, bracing breath, draw your short sword, and charge straight at the brutes between you and the slaves, hollering at the top of your lungs. Taken by surprise, the bugbears give way, and you sail right past them all, including the leader.

You find yourself in the midst of the slaves. "We might not be free," one of them says, "but we can keep you from suffering our fate!"

The crying boy lunges toward you. The lock on his shackles is the kind of cheap gadget you used to practice picking when you were his age. You slap it on the ground three times in just the right spots, and it springs open.

The boy's mother gasps and shoves the boy into your hands. "Take him!" she begs you. "Let him be free!"

You take off along the docks. The bugbears shout after you, but the other slaves spread out and slow them down with the chains that run between them.

You duck into one of Skullport's twisting alleys and lose yourself in the city. After a short while, you are so lost that you can't imagine anyone could find you.

You're also amazed to find that the boy has quieted down all on his own. You consider bringing him with you as you go hunting for the baby griffon, but you realize that hauling a kid into the Thieves' Guild with you is a recipe for getting you both killed. You opt for the surface instead.

By the time you find your way back to Waterdeep, the boy has fallen asleep in your arms. You see Jaulso waiting for you, sitting in a chair by the front door to your place. She's not happy.

"What happened?" she demands.

You do your best to explain everything, and the civilar nods along for a while. Then she holds up her hand for you to stop rambling.

"You're telling me you saved this kid rather than going to find a stolen baby griffon owned by a lord of Waterdeep?"

You start to stammer out an excuse, but she cuts you off again.

"Clearly I misjudged you." She stands and gives you an odd smile. "You're all right after all."

With that, she strolls off into a new day in Waterdeep, leaving you to head inside your place and lay the boy down to sleep.

THE END

I don't want to have anything to do with Skullport, pirates, or baby griffons," you tell Volo. "But if I don't find that little beast, I'm going to have to leave town!"

Volo pats you on the shoulder. "Now, that's not such a bad thing, is it? Do you have anything tying you to Waterdeep? Friends? Family? A magical compulsion?"

You shake your head.

Volo flashes a grin. "Then might I suggest the lure of the open road? I've traveled Faerûn from one end to the other, and it's filled with delights of all sorts. In fact . . ." He reaches into a bag on the seat next to him and pulls out a handful of freshly printed tomes. "I've written a number of guidebooks that could help you on your way."

You sigh and start rummaging through the titles. *Dungeonology*? You've always fancied becoming an adventurer. . . .

THE END

It takes you a while to find the Xanathar's home, mostly because you don't want to ask anyone where it is for fear of getting yourself in trouble again. It seems like the creature's very name is poison in this town, at least for anyone working outside the Thieves' Guild.

There are only so many well-appointed houses in Skullport, though, so it doesn't take you long to narrow down which ones are sufficiently swanky to belong to someone powerful enough to run the largest criminal organization in town. You skulk around the dark streets and alleys in the finest neighborhood in Skullport, peering through various windows at their occupants, until you spot a gigantic eyeball floating around inside one of the largest homes.

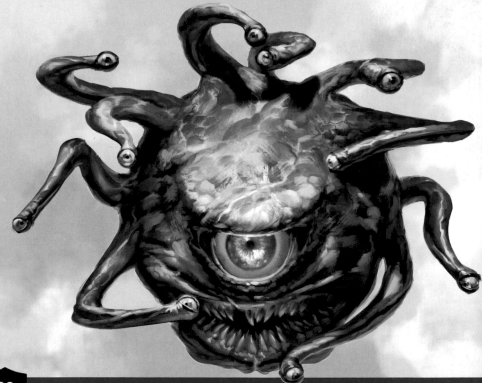

You find yourself a quiet spot across the street and sit tight. You wait until it seems as if everyone in the Xanathar's mansion has gone to bed, and then you slip through an open window into a pitch-black room. You let your eyes adjust to the darkness before you venture farther.

Now, where would I hide a baby griffon? is what you're thinking when you see a large pair of wings fluttering on the other side of the room. You realize that it's the baby griffon, and it's moving in its sleep!

You slink over to snatch up the little critter and run for it, but before you get halfway there, the lights in the room flare to life. You find yourself standing in the center of a wood-paneled office with polished marble floors. The Xanathar himself is in the room with you, floating over from the corner in which he was lying in wait.

"Welcome to my home, thief," the beholder says.

You open your mouth to explain yourself, but he cuts you off with a bitter chuckle. "You think I'm so stupid that I wouldn't expect the City Watch to send someone down here to find me? The only problem is I'm a wee bit insulted they only sent one person. And just a lowly halfling at that."

Turn to page 92 . . .

You're so disgusted by the idea of people owning and selling other people—especially children—that you draw your short sword and charge straight at the bugbears. You slash and stab left and right, raising blood wherever your blade lands.

Startled by the ferocity of your attack, the bugbears stagger backward, flinching away from your blade—all but the leader. You sprint up to him, and he chops at you with his spiked club. You dodge the blow by diving toward him, and you drive your blade into his thigh.

The leader howls in pain and hops away from you, screaming for the other bugbears to help him. They rally to his call, but as the bugbears close ranks around you, the slaves join your struggle! They swing their chains about them, using them as weapons, and they drive the bugbears back—except for a particularly slow one, who goes down with a large bruise to the side of his head.

One bugbear steps up and swings his club at the mother of the boy you heard crying. She lashes out with her chain and snares his club with the links. Then she yanks backward with all her might, pulling the weapon from his hands.

The slaves roar in triumph and press their advantage. The

84

bugbear leader falls to his knees, his injured leg no longer able to hold his weight.

You leap forward and press your blade to his throat. "Call them off!" you shout, hoping he can understand you.

His eyes open wide, and he shouts something at the other bugbears in their harsh tongue. The rest of them back away from the slaves, giving them a respectful distance. It won't last long, though. You need to move fast.

You spot a ring of keys on the leader's belt, and you tear them free and toss them to the mother. She unlocks her son's shackles first and then sets about releasing the rest of her fellow slaves.

The boy races over and throws his arms around you. He's crying again, but these are tears of joy.

Turn to page 93…

You decide to make your way over to the Thieves' Guild and see if you can spot the one-eyed floating beast there—and maybe the poor little griffon he's supposedly stolen. The building that houses the guild sits in a surprisingly decent part of town for how much crime runs through it. It seems that—at least in Skullport—crime pays rather well, and no one's about to question how brazenly well it does.

You stake the place out for a bit, but you don't see any sign of a beholder floating into or out of the place. Mind flayers? Check. Dark elves? Check. Even a trio of kobolds looking for trouble. But no one that looks anything like the Xanathar.

You start to wonder if the beholder was somehow dethroned. Could there be a new Xanathar in town? One who has legs?

Your feet are starting to get sore when you feel something sharp poke you between your ribs.

"Don't move," a voice orders in your ear.

You didn't get to live this long by not listening to people with a knife in your side. You freeze and wait for further instructions.

"What are you doing here?" the voice asks.

"That's the Thieves' Guild across the street, right?"

"And?"

You decide that whoever has you at their mercy doesn't need the whole truth of the matter. "I thought maybe I'd like to join."

"Are you a thief?"

That would seem obvious, but you don't wish to argue the point. You give your questioner a firm nod.

"Then you don't have much of a choice. You either join the Thieves' Guild or you leave."

"Then I suppose I'll leave." You try to turn around, but the knife digs further between your ribs.

"It's too late for that, I'm afraid," the person tells you.

"Don't tell me it's too late to join as well."

"That's up to you. You always have choices, as long as you still draw breath. Are you willing to pledge your life to the Thieves' Guild?"

"Of course!" you say. "If that's what it takes to keep breathing, I'm all for it."

You feel the knife slide all the way between your ribs and find your heart.

"That's too bad," your killer drawls in your ear. "I'm part of the Assassins' Guild."

THE END

I have had enough!" you shout. You feint at Heleen and then drive your knife straight into Fundunsun's chest.

The deep gnome gurgles in pain and surprise and clutches at the handle of your blade. He staggers backward, wrenching the knife from your grasp.

This leaves you defenseless against Heleen. She screeches in horror at what you've done and then stabs you in the midriff with her dagger.

It feels as if you've been punched in the stomach, and you collapse to the floor. A moment later, a flying bottle smashes against the side of your head and knocks you unconscious.

You awaken amid the wreckage of the brawl later, cold and aching with tiny winged creatures dancing across your eyelids.

"You big 'uns sure take a long time dying," the creature says as she moves down and starts going through your pockets. You lack the strength to brush her away.

THE END

The wound in your side is just too much to bear. Without treating it, you're sure to bleed out soon. If you stay to fight, you're doomed.

You steel yourself for one last trick. You feint at Heleen's bad side, and when she moves to protect it, you dash past her on the other side. She takes a swing at you, but you're already out of reach.

"Stop that thief!" Fundunsun shouts, but it's too late for anyone to manage it. You charge out onto the pier and dive straight over the edge. You take a big last breath before you disappear beneath the Sargauth's chilly black surface.

You swim as deep and as far as possible until your lungs can no longer hold out. When you can't take it any longer, you struggle back up to the surface and emerge gasping for precious air.

Glancing back, you see that you're far from the tavern now, well out of the range of anyone standing on the pier—even if they were bearing a bow. Unfortunately, that also puts you far past any way to return to Skullport.

Injured as you are, you can't fight the river's strong current. Instead, you concentrate on staying afloat and let the river have you. It sweeps you farther from Skullport, drawing you straight toward what appears to be the solid wall of the cavern's side.

Not wanting to wind up pinned against the wall, you start to swim away from it as hard as you can. The wound in your side shoots pain with every stroke, and all your efforts do little to slow your progress toward your inevitable doom.

As the wall fast approaches, you brace yourself for the unavoidable impact.

Instead, in the blink of an eye, you pass through some kind of a magic portal in the wall! You wind up somewhere else entirely, far from Skullport and beneath an open sky. The stars twinkle down at you, and you take a moment to cheer your incredible luck.

The water here is warmer and tastes of salt. You spy a tree-lined shore in the distance, and you make for it as best you can. Some endless amount of time later, you collapse on a sandy beach.

You soon realize you're alone and lost on some distant shoreline, far from help and home. But wherever you are, at least you'll die free.

THE END

Just don't hurt it," you say about the baby griffon.

The beholder laughs. "I got no reason to harm a feather on its head. I'm going to treat it better than I treat my own ungrateful offspring. We're going to be best friends." He gestures toward the still-sleeping young griffon. "I could sell this critter back to Lord Silverhand, but what would I get out of it? A sack of gold? A favor from a lord? Hah!"

He reaches over with one of his eyestalks and caresses the crest of the griffon's neck. "Now, I hold on to it, train it so one of my lieutenants can ride it? That's two points in my favor. Not only do I keep the Open Lord of Waterdeep from having a griffon mount, I get to use the critter for the Thieves' Guild instead."

"Smart," you say grudgingly.

"I like you, kid," the beholder says. "You got guts coming into my house like this. So I'm going to give you a choice. You can join my little operation, or you can die."

He narrows all eleven of his eyes at you. "What's it gonna be?"

Join the Thieves' Guild. Turn to page 94 . . .
Save the griffon! Turn to page 98 . . .
Attack the Xanathar! Turn to page 108 . . .

The bugbears slink off to lick their wounds. You look at the slaves and realize that they're weak and underfed. If they don't leave Skullport right now, they're sure to be recaptured—by those same bugbears or someone else.

Some of the now ex-slaves are scared to leave with you, thinking that you're going to claim them as your property. The boy cries, "Never! Heroes don't own slaves!"

The laughter from the others breaks the tension, and they all agree to follow you out of Skullport. You lead them back up to the surface by the fastest route you know.

When you reach Waterdeep, you realize that Jaulso will be furious with you for saving slaves rather than that baby griffon. You tell the ex-slaves that you're one of them now, and together you strike out from Waterdeep for parts unknown, to find your fortune.

THE END

It's hard to turn down a lethal monster—who also happens to be a powerful criminal overlord—when he makes you an offer like that. In fact, you don't see any wiggle room out of this at all.

"Sign me up," you say with as much enthusiasm as you can muster.

The Xanathar smiles at you, and you can see that you've made the right decision—at least for the moment. The beholder would have killed you on the spot if you refused him, and he has at least eleven different ways to manage it, all in the blink of an eye.

With that settled for now, the Xanathar gazes down at the sleeping baby griffon, and that same smile he flashed at you suddenly makes your blood run cold. You recognize what you didn't see hidden behind it while you were so relieved that you weren't going to die right away: hunger. Not for the griffon itself but for the power it represents.

"Of course, I can't simply trust someone who declares their loyalty to me under such circumstances," the beholder says with a wide, toothy smirk. "You're going to have to prove yourself to me."

"Of course," you say, trying to suppress a tremor of fear in your voice. You knew it couldn't be that easy. "What do you want from me?"

The Xanathar floats in your direction, his shadow falling over you as he looms overhead. "I need you to go get the trainer I lined up for this little critter and bring him to me. He works for Lord Silverhand at the moment, but he's ready to trade up to our side — as long as we can get him out of there without anyone trying to stop him."

You swallow hard, wondering exactly what Laeral Silverhand might do to you if she catches you in cahoots with the Xanathar rather than just with your hand in her pocket — which was bad enough. But you realize you have no choice. This is the only way you're getting out of Skullport alive.

There have to be worse things than being the stooge of a horrible monster bent on warping Waterdeep to his own ends. Right? After all, the Xanathar must have hundreds of thieves in his guild. At least you'll be in good — well, evil — company.

"Of course," you tell the Xanathar. "I'll leave right away. But, pardon me for asking, couldn't you just find someone else to train the griffon?"

The beholder looks at you as though you're the biggest fool he's ever hired. "How many people do you know that have any idea how to train a griffon? It's not like breaking a horse."

"And you don't think that Lord Silverhand or any of her

people are going to try to stop me from taking this trainer away from her manor?"

The Xanathar laughs. "I didn't say that at all. This isn't a simple errand. It requires a bit of discretion on your part to go smoothly. If Lord Silverhand somehow discovers what you're up to, you tell her to consider letting the trainer go with you as an act of charity toward the critter on her part. If she releases the trainer to us, the little guy will live a good, happy life with us. Otherwise, well, if I can't get any use out of it, no one will." The beholder's menace is unmistakable.

You nod, and the Xanathar calls for one of his lieutenants to bring you safely back to Waterdeep. It's still dark when you emerge inside the city, not so far from the mansion of Lord Silverhand.

"Good luck," the lieutenant says with a snicker before he disappears into the night.

For a moment, you struggle with what you should do. In the end, you stride up to the mansion's front door and knock hard on it. A moment later a butler arrives and asks what kind of business you might have with Lord Silverhand at this hour.

Betray the Xanathar! Turn to page 100 . . .
Ask for the trainer! Turn to page 105 . . .

You fake a coughing fit to hawk up as much phlegm as you can manage, and the Xanathar creeps closer to you. You wonder if you'd be better off if you managed to choke to death here and now. It might be better than going through with what you have planned.

You don't see any better options, though, and you steel yourself to do what you must. When the Xanathar floats lower to peer at you, you stand up and spit straight in his central eye.

As the beholder squawks in outrage, using his eyestalks to wipe his gigantic eye clean, you dash toward the sleeping griffon and gather it in your arms. Unfortunately, this startles the young griffon awake, and it flings its wings wide. This movement knocks over a nearby lantern, spraying flaming oil all over the Xanathar's office. That sets the beholder's desk on fire, and he backs away from it and screams for help to put the flames out.

You need to leave before anyone arrives to fight the fire. If the Xanathar somehow survives this, he's sure to take his pains out on you. You get a better grip on the griffon, holding it around its middle despite its squawking, and look for a way out. At the moment, anything will do!

You charge toward the nearest window and leap through it—unaware that it looks out over a several-story drop! As you fall toward your death, the griffon unfurls its wings and begins desperately flapping as hard as it can.

The little griffon's efforts only slow your descent at first, but as you dangle below the beast, you shout at it to try harder. It replies by glaring down at you and unleashing an ear-splitting screech.

By now, you've made it out over the river, and half the town is staring up at you. Rather than let the griffon shake you off, you clamber up its lion-like leg and sit squarely on its back, right between its wings.

"Please!" you shout at it, begging it to take mercy on you. "I'm here to save you!"

The griffon bends its neck all the way back around to stare at you with its eagle eyes, and you freeze, unsure what it might do next.

Turn to page 102 . . .

You clear your throat and tell the butler, "I'm here on urgent business, and I need to speak with Lord Silverhand at once."

The butler does not seem impressed, and you can hardly blame him. Even on your best day, you wouldn't look like the sort of person who has business with the Open Lord of Waterdeep. After what you've been through today, you probably look worse than a gutter rat.

"Concerning what matter?" he asks.

You hesitate for a moment, wondering if you should just turn around and leave, but you realize that you have to say something to this man if you wish to gain an audience with Laeral Silverhand. At least it would beat screaming for the Open Lord at the top of your lungs. "A missing griffon," you say.

The butler gives you a ferocious scowl, and for a moment you wonder if he's going to slam the door in your face and call for the City Watch. Instead, he escorts you into the manor, and you do your best to ignore the ugly glares he gives you. A moment later, you find yourself in a richly appointed office, where Laeral Silverhand is waiting for you, despite the late hour.

"My apologies, my lord," you say with a shallow bow. "I have done as you wished."

"You managed to find my griffon?"

You nod, reluctant to say more.

"I notice you have no griffon with you."

You wince. "No, my lord, but I know where it is."

Laeral frowns and then slouches in the overstuffed chair behind her desk. "Please tell me this isn't some kind of ploy to pluck gold from my pocket. Again."

"No!" you say. "I risked life and limb to find the creature for you, and I saw him with my own two eyes."

"Her," the lord says. "You saw her." She sighs. "I suppose it was too much to ask for you to bring her back with you."

"I couldn't have pried her free from the Xanathar's clutches with anything less than a full platoon of the City Watch," you say.

"Then that's what you shall have."

You shake your head. "I'm good at finding things, my lord, not leading soldiers. The Xanathar thinks I'm working for him, that I'm here to steal away with the griffon's trainer."

"Then why aren't you doing just that?" the lord asks, bemused. "Are you somehow more afraid of me than you are of him?"

"Not at all," you say. "I just couldn't stand the idea of such a magnificent creature being enslaved to the whims of the Xanathar for the rest of her life."

Turn to page 113 . . .

You reach out with a tentative hand and give the griffon a reassuring stroke between its ears. It draws in a large breath, and you prepare for it to bite you in half with its vicious beak. Then the beast lets out a relieved sigh instead.

You can't help but follow suit.

You guide the griffon back toward the hole through which you fell into the Sargauth, high in the cavern. It's hard to find it in the darkness, but eventually you locate the hole and coax the creature into zooming up it.

A few terrifying moments later, you find yourself bursting through the hatchway you were pushed down, startling the hooded man, who's been snoring nearby.

You nudge the griffon up into the open sky, and the creature climbs so high that you can see all of Waterdeep spread out beneath you. A few lights flicker here and there in the predawn darkness.

Bring the griffon to the lord. Turn to page 118 . . .
Flee town. Turn to page 121 . . .

Your blade sings through the air toward your target and strikes true! Unfortunately, your sword bounces off the beholder's tough skin. You catch it as it plummets back to the ground, but the effort places you directly below the creature in easy range.

The Xanathar plucks your knife from his central eye with a horrific scream, and you stagger backward, stunned by his agony. He keeps his main eye closed tight, although gigantic tears seep from it and splash onto his desk. The rest of his eyes all turn toward you at once.

"That hurt!" the Xanathar bellows.

A bloodred ray fires from one of the beholder's eyes, and it catches the hand in which you're holding your short sword. You can feel the bones crunch together as if your hand had been placed in a vise, and you drop your blade as you yelp in agony.

Grab the griffon and run! Turn to page 110 . . .
Surrender! Turn to page 116 . . .

A ctually," you tell the butler, "I'm here on business with the griffon trainer."

The butler narrows his eyes at you suspiciously. You worry that he might call for the guards. But after a moment, he nods at you. "I do hope the trainer is expecting you at such a late hour."

"So do I," you say as you follow the butler into the manor. "I'm working with the City Watch to help find the griffon, and I have some questions for the trainer."

"Ah, so you're that halfling. Very well." The butler takes you through a series of passages that lead to a room adjoining a wide balcony on which someone has set up a stable with a gigantic nest made of sticks and straw in the middle of it. He knocks on the door to the room, and a harried-looking man answers.

"Yes?" he says, irritated.

"Traynov? This halfling has some questions for you about the griffon." The butler nods to you with a distasteful sneer. You wave up at the man, who clearly doesn't recognize you or why you might darken his door at this time of night.

"A-all right," he says with guarded approval.

The butler gives the two of you a sad shake of his head. It's clear he doesn't care for either of you. "I'll leave you to your business."

Once the butler is gone, Traynov slips out of his room and hisses at you. "Who sent you?"

You hesitate for a moment, realizing that there's no turning back from this. Then you spit it out: "The Xanathar."

"Thanks be to the gods," Traynov exclaims. "I thought they'd abandoned me. If Lord Silverhand managed to figure out how I helped them steal the griffon, I'd wind up in chains for sure!"

He ducks back into his room and emerges a moment later with a bag full of his things slung over his shoulder. Slinking through the manor a different way than you came, you exit through a back door.

You bring Traynov down to Skullport and turn him over to the Xanathar, who cackles with glee. "You've done better than I'd hoped," he says. "Of course, the entire City Watch will be on the hunt for your hide now, but don't you worry about it. You're part of the Thieves' Guild of Waterdeep, and we protect our own."

"Does that protection extend to the streets of Waterdeep?"

The beholder grunts. "Don't go tempting fate just because you've been guilded. It's not like a wizard made you invulnerable. If Lord Silverhand sees you wandering around—or Civilar Jaulso—you might find you have the kind of problem the guild can't help you with."

"Isn't that what the guild is for?"

"We can break you out of jail. Bringing you back from the dead is a much bigger ask." The Xanathar turns all eleven of his eyes on you. "Let's talk about what we can do to make money off each other instead."

You shiver under the creature's gaze, but you don't object. He has a point. You sold him your soul, so you might as well get a good price for it.

THE END

You know that taking on a beholder is probably the stupidest thing you could do, but you can't leave the griffon here in the Xanathar's care. And even if you manage to get away with the griffon, the beholder is sure to kidnap the little creature again. You need to put an end to this threat now, no matter how risky such a move might be.

"So?" the Xanathar says.

You fiddle about for a bit, pretending you need more time to make up your mind. In fact, you're reaching for the knife hidden in a secret sheath on the back of your belt.

The beholder floats closer, looming as he focuses all eleven of his eyes on you, each of which could murder you in a different way. If he's trying to intimidate you, it's working. You suppress a shiver of fear.

"Well?" he says.

"Keep an eye peeled," you say to him, trying to draw him closer. You're probably going to get only one good shot at him, and you need to make it count. "That's such an odd expression, don't you think? I mean, who peels an eye? What, like an apple? Or an egg?"

The beholder squints at you with all of his eyes at once, unsure where you're going with your babbling. He floats toward you, putting him right where you want him. You whip out your knife and hurl it at his gigantic central eye in one swift move.

Your blade plunges straight into the massive orb, and the Xanathar screeches in horrible pain as he recoils from you. While the creature tries to extract your knife from his central eye with his eyestalks, you pull your short sword from its scabbard and leap toward him.

Despite the damage you've done to his central eye and how much pain he's in, the Xanathar still has ten other eyes to see you coming. He dodges out of the way of the first swing of your sword and then floats up toward the room's vaulted ceiling, putting him firmly out of your reach.

You realize then that you may have made a horrible—potentially fatal—mistake. You should have climbed on top of the creature while you had your chance.

Still, you've cast your dice. The Xanathar's sure to kill you as soon as he manages to yank your knife from his eye, so the only thing you can do is press your advantage while it lasts. You cock your arm and hurl your short sword up at the villainous beast with all of your might.

Turn to page 103...

Desperate, you charge toward the griffon. The Xanathar's screams have jolted the young creature awake, and it stares up at you in surprise. For an instant, you wonder if it might attack you with those lethal claws it has, but it gives you a hopeful look instead.

"It's all right," you tell it in what you hope is a soothing tone. "I'm here to rescue you."

It seems to understand that, and edges toward you.

Another ray fires from one of the beholder's eyes, and the floor beneath your feet disappears, nearly dropping you into the room below. You leap onto the pedestal the baby griffon is resting on, and you snatch the creature up with your uninjured arm. You hold it between you and the Xanathar, hoping that the beholder isn't willing to risk killing the griffon to reach you.

"Come on, little one," you urge the griffon as you jump from the pedestal and head to the window. "Let's go!"

"You think I'm going to let you get away with this?" the Xanathar says in a ferocious rage, his voice as edgy as shattered glass. "It's one thing to steal from me. We're all thieves down here. That's what we do. But no one hurts me and gets to live!"

"You might not have the final word on that," you say through teeth gritted in pain. You reach the window and look down at the dizzying drop below. You know you can't survive a fall like that. But maybe you don't have to.

You turn back and see the beholder floating toward you, and you know that he is set on killing you for sure.

There's no way for you're going to talk your way out of this one. If you don't make your move now, he will find the right angle with one of his eyestalks and take you down. The only thing stopping him from destroying you immediately is the fact that he'd probably kill the griffon at the same time. The moment you separate from his prized creature, you're doomed.

Keeping the griffon between the two of you, you work your way up onto the windowsill, never taking your gaze off the beholder.

You make up your mind about what you have to do. At least this way you won't give the Xanathar the satisfaction of killing you himself.

"I hope your eye rots out of your head," you say just before you tumble backward out the window, clutching the young griffon as you go.

The Xanathar shouts in protest, but it's too late for him to stop you. You black out before you reach the ground racing up at you.

Turn to page 119 . . .

The lord sends Jaulso and her Watchers to retrieve the baby griffon. Hours pass, and it is the middle of the day before Jaulso returns to the lord's mansion — with no griffon in sight.

"The Xanathar's home was there, just as the halfling said, but the griffon and its kidnapper were not." She turns to you. "They abandoned the place immediately after you left them. Are you so naive as to think they would trust you?"

"I'm doomed," you say. "The Thieves' Guild has it in for me, and the City Watch won't trust me either, I'm sure."

"Despite that, I trust you," Lord Silverhand says. "And I can always find a use for an honest thief."

Over the years, you help the lord foil all sorts of crazy plots against the people of Waterdeep. Several times, you manage to save her life.

Many years later, while trying to infiltrate the Thieves' Guild to find a powerful amulet they have come into possession of, you discover a full-grown griffon that has been in the employ of the Xanathar for decades. You free the creature from its servitude under the master of the Thieves' Guild, and because it is still bonded to Lord Silverhand, it returns to her immediately.

Reunited with the griffon, Lord Silverhand's first order of business is to ride straight into Skullport and tear the Xanathar's home right down to its foundation. The beholder is never heard from again.

THE END

Lord Silverhand expresses her undying gratitude to you and assures you that there's a permanent place for you on her staff should you be inclined to take such a job. "I'm sure I can find a use for someone with your rare and valuable talents," she says without a trace of irony.

You wonder how many people a woman like Lord Silverhand might have working for her in similar positions, but once you think about it for a moment, you realize that the Xanathar's sure to be furious with you. There's no place in Waterdeep that could be safe for you, unless you refuse to leave the lord's estate for the rest of your life. Even then, you would likely be flirting with a horrible fate.

You don't see her gratitude extending to you for the decades of life you hope to have left. "I think I should be on my way," you tell her. "Far, far away."

"There's no need for that," Lord Silverhand says with a knowing look. "If you're afraid of the Thieves' Guild, I have the magical means to disguise you permanently."

You gaze out the window of the lord's home and realize that there's no place in Faerûn you'd rather be than right here in Waterdeep. You could run, but you don't know where to. This is your home, and you don't want to be forced to leave it. "All right," you say.

Hours later, you stroll out of Lord Silverhand's mansion, literally a new person. You'd wanted to become someone who can go wherever they want, moving between the wealthy homes of the Sea Ward and the gutters of the worst parts of Waterdeep at will. There's only one person you know who fits that bill, and now you look, and sound, exactly like him.

You bump into a member of the City Watch as you stroll down the street. The soldier turns and glares at you for a moment before her face breaks into a smile. "Volo!" she says to you. "Always a pleasure!"

"The pleasure is mine, I assure you," you tell the Watcher. You adjust your satchel, which jingles a bit from the sack of gold coins Lord Silverhand gave you, and you head on your way.

If you have to live as someone else, it might as well be Volothamp Geddarm. You could get used to this.

THE END

You throw yourself on your knees in front of the Xanathar to beg for his mercy. "I'm so sorry!" you tell him, your voice cracking in desperation. "I was cornered! I never thought I could actually harm someone as powerful as you!"

"Well, you did a fine job despite that!" the Xanathar growls at you.

Hope rises in your heart, based entirely on the fact that you're not already dead. If he wanted to kill you for your transgression, you think it would have happened by now.

"Just let me know how I can make it up to you." You grovel as hard as you can. "I'll do anything. Take you to the civilar who set me after you? Done! Deliver to you the lord of Waterdeep who owned your griffon? Done! Whatever you wish! Done!"

The Xanathar snickers at your performance, and you open your eyes to gaze up at him as he glares down at you. He knows you can't give him the things you're promising, but he seems to appreciate the fact that you're willing to try.

"Very well," the Xanathar says begrudgingly. "You have earned both my anger and my mercy."

You throw up your arms in gratitude. "Thank you!" you shout, still surprised that you remain alive. "You won't regret this. I'll be your devoted servant for the rest of my miserable life!"

"Yes, you will," the Xanathar says as he focuses all of his eyestalks on you. They bob and weave like a nest of furious snakes, and you find yourself almost hypnotized by their movement.

"What do you wish for me to do, sir?" you say. "Just say the word, and I will leap into action for you."

"I have one request," the beholder says. "Hold still . . ."

You look up at the creature, gazing right into his malevolent central eye, and all hope shrivels inside you. You should have tried to run, but now it's too late to even give that a shot.

A blackish ray leaps from the end of one of the Xanathar's eyestalks, and it catches you in it like a moth in a lantern's light. A chill runs straight through you as the ray pierces your body and snuffs out your life. Your heart stops beating, your breath catches in your lungs, and your vision tunnels down to absolute darkness.

"Thank you," the Xanathar says, followed by the last words you will ever hear. "That will be all."

THE END

You decide against bringing the griffon to Jaulso, convinced that the civilar would try to take all the credit for your hard work. And where would that leave you?

It seems only right that you bring the griffon directly back to the lord who lost it. Jaulso didn't risk her life to save the griffon, did she? And after all you've been through, you deserve to bask in Lord Silverhand's gratitude directly.

You give the griffon its head, and sure enough, you don't have to even tell it where to go. It flies straight to the mansion of its master, Lord Laeral Silverhand, and spirals down toward it out of the open sky. You land on a broad balcony that features a gigantic nest, and the creature begins squawking at the top of its lungs.

Soon enough, Lord Silverhand bursts out of the manor and sprints right for the griffon. From the way the creature flies straight toward her embrace, you know you did the right thing by bringing the tyke here.

Turn to page 114 . . .

Y ou awaken in the softest bed you've ever known. A bright ray of sunshine streams through the tall window nearby, and you realize you're no longer in Skullport.

You're in a hospital of some kind, and you're relieved that your hand no longer hurts so much. When you raise your arm to inspect it, though, you instantly see why: the hand is gone.

A nurse enters the room and fusses over you for a bit. You have lots of questions, but she refuses to answer any of them. Instead, she hands you a heavy sack of coins and an envelope that bears a note of gratitude from Lord Laeral Silverhand for "the happy return of my wonderful friend."

"This also came for you," she says as she hands you a folded note.

You unfold it and shiver in terror as you read the words scrawled there.

"You cannot escape me. Don't even try."

It's signed by the Xanathar.

THE END

As the young griffon circles above the city, you guide it north, and it gives in to your wishes. You have cousins who live near Baldur's Gate, and with any luck they'll welcome you with open arms.

By midday, the griffon tires and insists on landing. You're nervous about setting down in the open, but you don't see how you have much of a choice. You let the griffon take you to a bald-topped mountain and land on a wide and easy ledge near its summit.

Soon after, a piercing shriek rattles the clouds above. You race to the griffon, but it takes off into the sky, leaving you behind.

A moment later, the buffeting wind from a gigantic set of wings hits you with the force of a hurricane and knocks you to your knees. Once the wind subsides, something blots out the midday sun. You glance up to see a pair of wings stretched wide overhead. You cheer, thinking that the baby griffon is back to save you.

When the creature above you lands, though, the earth shudders, and you realize that this griffon is much larger than the one you came here with. You scramble backward on the seat of your pants and cast about for some means of escape from the gigantic beast.

There is nowhere to run. Not unless you want to throw yourself down the side of a mountain and take your chances with a likely fatal fall.

What you wouldn't give right now for a ring of invisibility . . .

The griffon stamps toward you, and you realize that this is the end.

Then the baby griffon comes screeching down out of the sky, putting itself between the big griffon and you. The larger creature stops itself from striking at you and caws at the younger one instead. The little one leaps forward and nuzzles the bigger one, and the full-grown griffon gives the smaller one a tender rub with its beak.

After a moment, the two griffons part, and the bigger creature gives you a respectful nod of its head.

"No trouble at all," you say, thrilled and terrified at the same time. "Happy to help!"

The two leap into the air and flap off into the distance. You wish you could follow them, but you'll have to settle for hiking toward Baldur's Gate instead.

THE END

The images in this book were created by Aaron R. Riley, Annie Stegg, Bryan Syme, Chris Seaman, Conceptopolis, Craig J. Spearing, David Hueso, E. W. Hekaton, Emily Fiegenschuh, Emrah Elmasli, Eric Belisle, Eva Widermann, Francis Tsai, Jason Juta, Julian Kok Joon Wen, Kieran Yanner, Klaus Pillon, Lars Grant-West, Lindsey Look, Marl A. Nelson, Mark Behm, Michael Berube, Mike Faille, Noah Bradley, Olga Drebas, Sam Burley, Scott Murphy, Shawn Wood, Steve Prescott, Steven Belledin, Tyler Jacobson, Vincent Proce, Wayne England, William O'Connor, and Zoltan Boros.

The cover illustrations were created by Jesper Ejsing and Mark A. Nelson.

CANDLEWICK
ENTERTAINMENT

First U.S. edition 2018
Library of Congress Catalog Card Number pending
ISBN 978-1-5362-0243-4 (hardcover) 978-1-5362-0066-9 (paperback)
18 19 20 21 22 23 WKT 10 9 8 7 6 5 4 3 2 1
Printed in Shenzhen, Guangdong, China
Candlewick Press, 99 Dover Street, Somerville, Massachusetts 02144
visit us at www.candlewick.com

Don't miss the other Dungeons & Dragons® Endless Quest® titles!

Escape the Underdark
Into the Jungle
Big Trouble

Or these Dungeons & Dragons titles available from Candlewick Press:

Monsters and Heroes of the Realms
Dungeonology